SUPER MONSTA FRIENDS

WELCOME!

This Monsta World was created for
YOU to fill with **YOUR** hopes,
dreams, doodles, silliness, and creativity.
In Doodlandia, just like the "Real World,"
possibilities are endless, creativity is
awesome, boredom stinks,
and magic happens every day!
Welcome to YOUR Doodlverse.
Are you ready?

NEVER BE BORED AGAIN!

For BECKY, DYLAN & LOGAN
dream big

SWEET!!

Published by Scholastic Inc., *Publishers since 1920.* SCHOLASTIC and associated logos are trademarks and/or registered trademarks of Scholastic Inc.

The publisher does not have any control over and does not assume any responsibility for author or third-party websites or their content.

This book is a work of fiction. Names, characters, places, and incidents are either the product of the author's imagination or are used fictitiously, and any resemblance to actual persons, living or dead, business establishments, events, or locales is entirely coincidental.

ISBN 978-0-545-83965-5

10 9 8 7 6 5 4 3 2 1   16 17 18 19 20

Printed in Malaysia   106
First printing 2016

THIS BOOK BELONGS TO:

(doodle the first letter in your name)

(doodle your name in a fun way)

(give yourself a Monsta name)

(doodle your name in a fancy way)

MY biggest dream is . . .

(your age)

YAY!

doodle your pet (real or make-believe)

★ MY FiRST tiny DOODLE

doodle something super-small

BE ON THE LOOKOUT FOR TOP SECRET MESSAGES HIDDEN THROUGHOUT THE DOODLVERSE!

TOP SECRET! put your thumbprint somewhere on this page

doodle something that begins with the first letter in your name

doodle it!

SMACK!

AAAAHHHH!!!

fill in what Tazza says

Life is an
adventure.
Go LIVE it!

draw an exciting picture that
makes you think of an adventure ↗

This can only mean one thing,
the greatest adventure in all
the Doodlverse . . .

ROAD
TRIP!

Geehost is super-excited about his new phone!
Doodle and design his new phone. It has 3 buttons, a big screen, a camera, and an awesome case.

Booyah!!!

Copy this page and invite your parents on a road trip.
Fill in where you will be going, when you will leave, and
doodle some things you will see along the way.

You're invited on a
ROAD TRIP!

_____
where we are going

_____   _____
date we are leaving   date we are coming back

we can expect to see

DeeWee, like all Monstas, is a BIG dreamer and wants to visit the Statue of Doodlery.
What are some places you dream of visiting?

I dream of going to:

another state

I dream of going to:

a big city

My biggest dream is to go to:

doodle it!

a faraway country

YOU can do it!

draw an alien inside the rocket

small monsta BIG dreams

Make a list of things to take on a road trip.

DON'T FORGET

ROAD TRIP

draw them here

Don't forget the waffles!

TOP SECRET!
draw a supersecret thing you want to bring on the road trip, but *shhh!* It's your secret!

Sir Doodlot's Kingdom is a magical place full of fun, doodles, games, and more. Tazza has dreamed of going to Sir Doodlot's since he started collecting Doodlot's doodles.

doodle a fish

doodle a Monsta with 3 eyes

doodle a fancy letter

doodle a robot

doodle a castle

Fill the picture frames with fun doodles.

Doodle some things you collect in your house on the shelves below.

WHOA!

SDK

MY FAVORITE THING

↳doodle your favorite thing in your room↰

Percy Pencil is the mascot for Sir Doodlot's Kingdom.
Percy is always happy, full of magic, fun, and imagination.
Make drawings around Percy that make you happy.

TOP SECRET!
draw your favorite cool
pencil and eraser
somewhere on this page

PERCY PENCIL

If you created your own theme park, what would it be called? What would your mascot be?
Draw a fun mascot for your theme park.

Draw it on this base

AWESOME! I wanna go to your theme park!

_____
(name your theme park)

_____
(name your mascot)

Before the road trip begins, Tazza has to take his pet Puppicorn to the pet sitter. Help him get there by choosing a path—but watch out for doodle blocks along the way!

doodle a big Monsta blocking the path

doodle a stop sign

doodle a happy tree

FUN

doodle water

PET! PET!

TOP SECRET!
get your pet to walk
across this page or, even
better, lie on it!

doodle an acorn

Oh, no! Tazza overpacked!
Doodle the 10 suitcases he packed and some of the extra stuff inside them.

Help! Chomp is freaking out!
He can't seem to find his food for the road trip.
Can you find all his food before he eats this book?

OH! No! No! Nooooo!

Chomp's Missing Food

- [ ] Hot Dog
- [ ] Ice Cream Cone
- [ ] Pretzel
- [ ] Donut
- [ ] Fish
- [ ] Carrot
- [ ] Banana
- [ ] Hamburger
- [ ] Pizza
- [ ] Cotton Candy

check the boxes as you find them

MONSTA TOONAGE
A DOODLTOON

Hu-hu-hu . . . Wait. What?! You found all my FOOD?!?!

YOU'RE THE BEST!

yummy

Wow. . . That was so exhausting!!! I'm gonna sit here and eat this yummy strawberry, vanilla, nacho cheese, sprinkles, and hot dog ice cream cone! You mind packing for me?

draw all of Chomp's food you found

FREE TO BE ME!

↤ copy this page then cut along the dotted line ↦

Slogs enjoys every second of the day and all the unique Monsta friends he meets while on a road trip.

Draw words around the poster that make you unique. Celebrate YOUR awesomeness!

Slogs loves supersilly hats.
How silly a hat can you draw on Slogs for the trip?

TOP SECRET!
put a picture of you wearing your favorite hat on this page

doodle a background for Scoopie

← cut along the dotted line to make a poster →

TOP SECRET! write your biggest dream on the poster, so you can read it every day

Color in the drawing, tear it out once you've finished the whole book, and hang it in your room.

I'm away on a
ROAD TRIP!
be back soon

Make a fun door hanger for your room while you are away on your road trip.
Draw where you are going on your road trip in the blue box.

← cut along the dotted line →

Before we hit the road, let's add some cool drawings to Creely's Monstabego.

After you've designed the Monstabego, draw a few birds in the sky and some clouds shaped like animals.

TOP SECRET!
Run over this page with your bike, leaving a tire track. Write down the color and type of bike you have.

Super-excited to leave on their adventure, the Monstas review the map one last time.

The Booger-Picking Musuem

Largest Used Cotton Swab

Massive Monkey Man

Gross Gorge

Mount Monstmore

Largest Ball of Belly Button Lint

Magical Mystical Mountains

Stinkiest Sock Superstore

Milkshake Mountain

The Yelling Yellow Yeti

FINISH

Sir Doodlot's Kingdom

Mermaid Mountain

Melvin's Magical Myth Store

MELVIN'S

Willie's Weird Wardrobe Factory

Yay!!

Pete's Pencil Palace

Ernie's Eraser Emporium

SDK

map of the
DOODLVERSE

With so much to see along the way to Sir Doodlot's Kingdom, the Monstas finish packing the Monstabego and hit the open road.

START

The World's Largest Splinter Ever Removed Memorial

Cotton Candy Caverns

Ms. Monty's Mythical Farm

Fluffiest Cat in the Doodiverse

Rainbow Arch

Squirmin's Gummy Worm Factory

Bigfoot's Big Toe

Great Food Plains

draw the state you live in

Largest Hot Dog Known to Monstakind

Giant Ice Cream Scoop Monsta Park

Chocolate Cup Canyon

list the states you have visited

Tazza and Zippy love playing I Spy on a road trip.
Look around you and doodle the things
Tazza and Zippy spy.

I spy with my Monsta eye something longer than my foot.

COOL

I spy with my Monsta eye
something that could fit on my finger.

I spy with my Monsta eye
something blue.

I spy with my
BIG Monsta eye
something floating!

I spy with my Monsta eye something round.

I spy with my Monsta eye a funny word.

On the way to the World's Largest Splinter Ever Removed Memorial, the Monstas drove past some fun things.
Draw them in the spaces below.

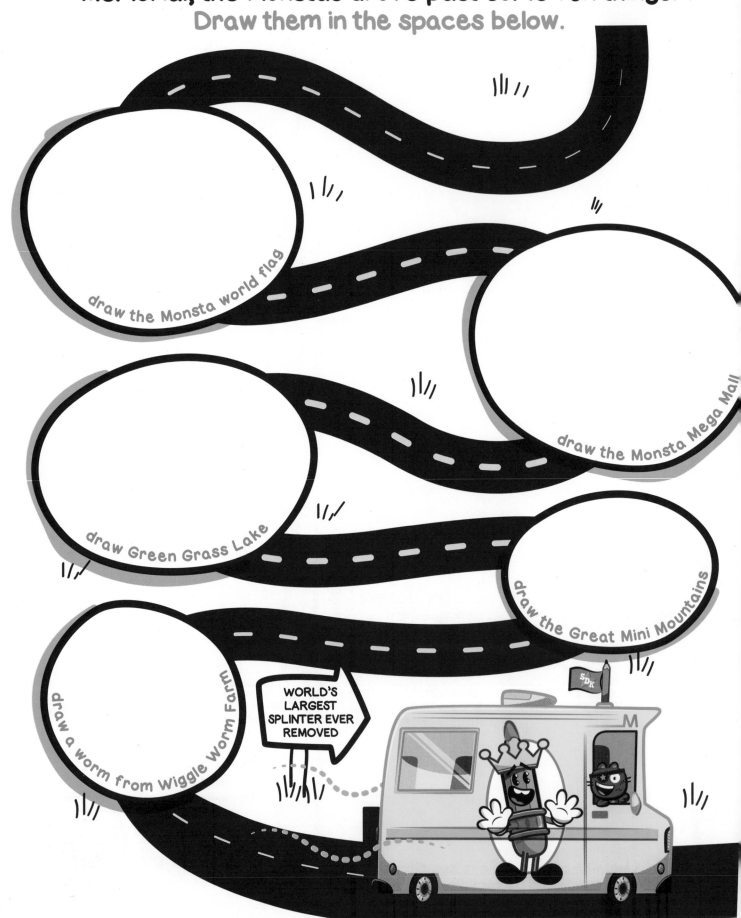

draw the Monsta world flag

draw the Monsta Mega Mall

draw Green Grass Lake

draw the Great Mini Mountains

draw a worm from Wiggle Worm Farm

WORLD'S LARGEST SPLINTER EVER REMOVED

The Super Monsta Friends all gathered around The World's Largest Splinter Ever Removed Memorial for a picture.
Draw what you think the splinter would look like.

FUN FACT

The splinter was so large the wood was used to build four Monsta houses. Ouch!

TOP SECRET!
make a drawing on this page using your finger

It's time for another joke with Rainer...

It all started when I was walking through Doodlandia forest, when suddenly from behind a bush I heard this strange sniffling sound like something was crying . . .

doodle the scene from Rainer's story

VOTE
check one ☐ good joke ☐ bad joke

All this driving has made me so hungry! Let's play Build-A-Cone!

BUILD-A-CONE

RULES OF THE GAME:
1. Player One thinks of a word, phrase, or sentence.
2. Player Two tries to guess it by suggesting letters.
3. If Player Two misses a letter, Player One doodles parts to Chomp's cone.
4. Chomp's cone is made up of 6 parts:
   cone, ice cream, sprinkles, a hot dog, nacho cheese, and a cherry
5. To win, Player Two must guess the correct word before all of Chomp's cone is doodled.

this is what Chomp's cone looks like

m o n s t a

guesses & misses

zpreh

guesses & misses

BUILD-A-CONE

guesses & misses

guesses & misses

Seriously! What's taking so long?! I'm starving!

Geehost and DeeWee have taken some really neat pics on their road trip.
Draw them.

draw something you see out your window

Draw your smile

Say MONSTA!

TOP SECRET! Be sneaky and photobomb someone's picture. Bonus points if you don't get caught!

draw something you can sit inside

draw your parents

draw something you see with four legs

doodle your favorite candy on the walls of Cotton Candy Caverns

Cotton Candy Caverns is a magical yummy wonderland made of all kinds of sugary goodness.
Draw the different candies that are found in the caverns.

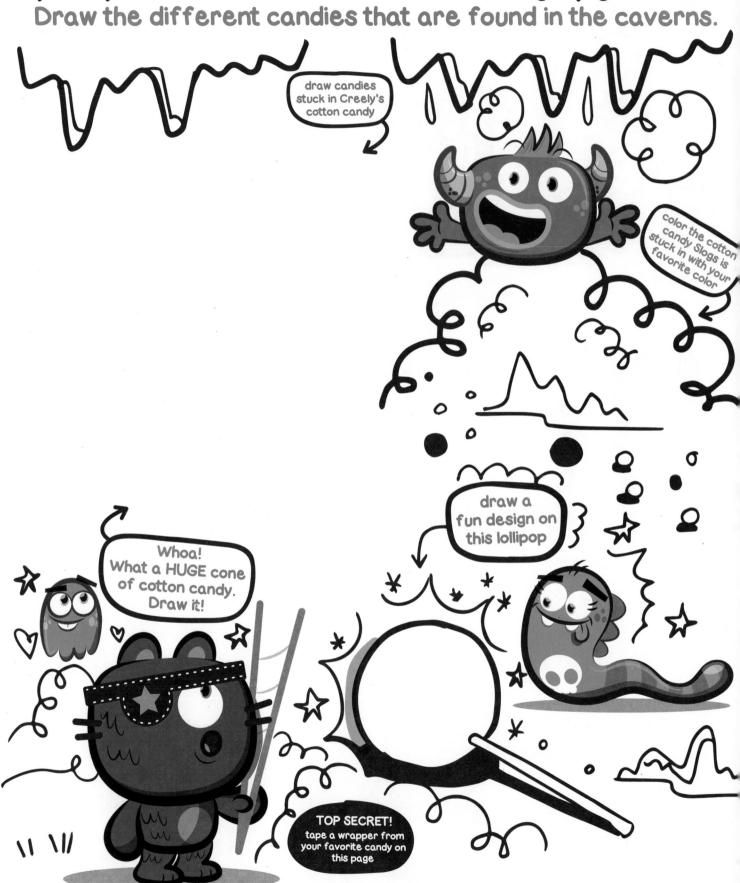

Doodle your favorite things that begin
with the letter in the boxes below.

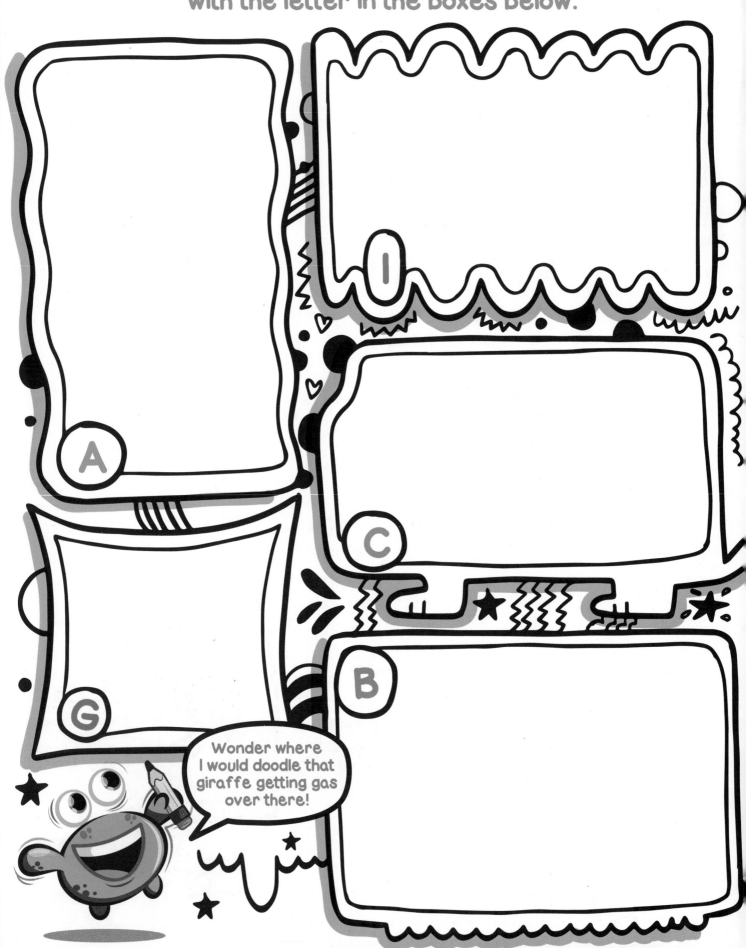

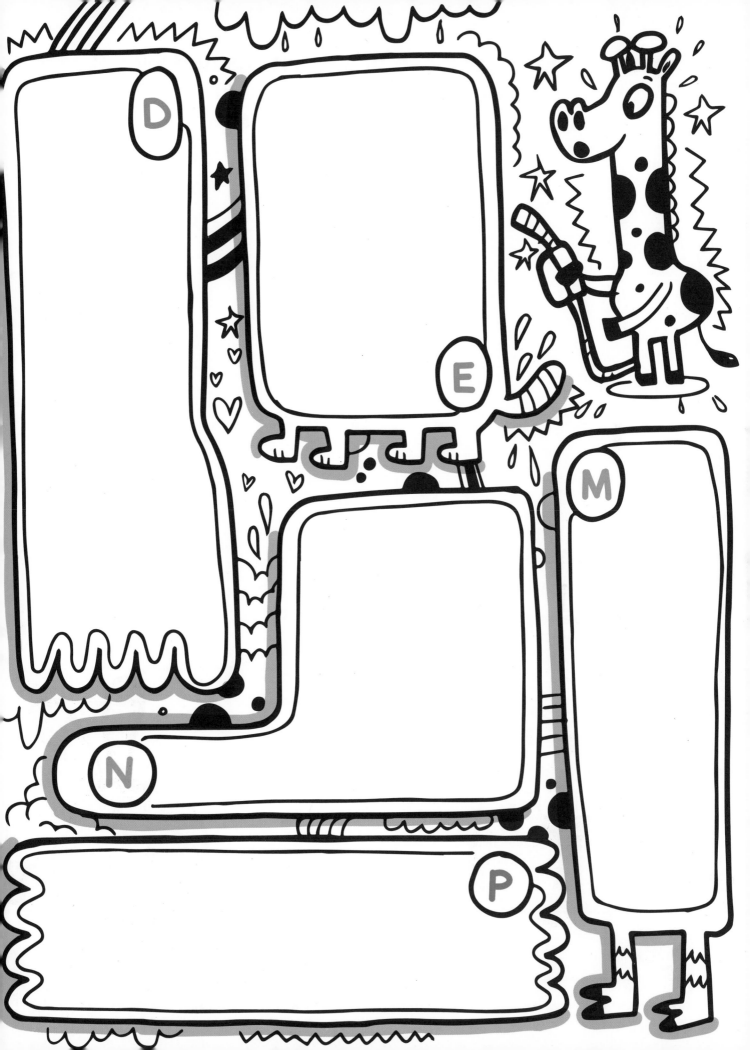

Rainer and Lovegood are great friends and love playing silly games during the road trip like stacking up items they can find in the Monstabego.

Can you doodle the items to create a giant stack without it falling over?

the stack has:
6 pots
4 bowls
3 sandwiches
5 spoons
1 toaster

← copy this page then cut along the dotted line →

DeeWee and Slogs are Monsta BFFs and always help each other out. Doodle words around the poster about your BFF and what makes them special.
Don't forget to tell them how awesome they are!

draw a roadside background

Running on Empty!
(fill in the missing words)

With all the noise inside the Monstabego, Creely didn't hear

the _____ buzzer going off, telling him the tank was
        (adjective)

on _____. Next thing he knew, the Monstabego was
   (something you yell)

out of gas, and they were stranded on the side of the road

without a _____ in sight.
          (a thing you can hold)

"Great! What are we going to do without_____!"
                                        (a thing you can drink)

Creely said.

"Friends help friends!" Lovegood exclaimed.

After a quick huddle around the _____,Whiz
                                (a place you sit)

decided he would go find _____ to fill up the
                         (a thing you can drink)

_____.
(type of container)

"It's great having such awesome Monsta friends,"

Creely exclaimed while _____.
                       (a movement you do)

Whiz is the fastest Monsta, but he's a bit silly.
Help Whiz get to the gas station quickly and save the day for his friends.

draw an animal that lives in the woods

draw a tree in the way

draw a huge rock in the road

draw a wrong way sign

GAS

GAS

TOP SECRET!
write down your favorite road trip snack that you can pick up at a gas station

Now that the Monstas are back on the road, it's time to complete the alphabet by doodling your favorite things that start with each letter.

draw unicorns around Lovegood so she can hide in a unicorn crowd using her new disguise

Lovegood is so excited to visit Ms. Monty's Mythical Farm with her friends. It's the home of some of the most magical creatures in all the Doodlverse.

As you explore the farm, be on the lookout for hidden places to draw.

Let's make some magic!

BUILD -A- UNICORN

RULES OF THE GAME:
1. Player One thinks of a word, phrase, or sentence.
2. Player Two tries to guess it by suggesting letters.
3. If Player Two misses a letter, Player One doodles parts of the unicorn.
4. The unicorn is made up of 6 parts:
   head, body, legs, tail, ears, and horn
5. To win, Player Two must guess the correct word before the whole unicorn is doodled.

Like this

h _ _ p p _

guesses & misses

hseitucp

guesses & misses

BUILD -A- UNICORN

guesses & misses

guesses & misses

I believe in magic!

Yay

Did you know Bigfoot had big dreams to be an artist and practiced drawing on his big toe?

I BELIEVE IN MAGIC!

↤ copy this page then cut along the dotted line to make a poster ↦

Sometimes our dreams seem impossible, maybe even make-believe.
Creely believes anything is possible with enough hard work,
a happy attitude, and some magic.
Doodle some of your dreams inside the big foot. Don't stop believin'!

The biggest, fluffiest cat in the Doodiverse calls Paws Passage her home and doesn't do a very good job of cleaning up after herself.

Doodle the cat mess she has left. It can include toys, food bowls, brushes, and even hair balls!

doodle a super-colorful cat paw

Cats are super-lazy and just sleep the day away.
Draw activities that you can do instead of being lazy.

Let's do something right meow!

Life is Monsta fun!

Draw your pet and its toys.
If you don't have a pet, make up a pet that you wish you had.

Whatta pet!

↳ write the name of your pet ↰

TOP SECRET!
put a picture of your
pet on this page

Oh, no! There is a huge artist's block in the road stopping the Monstas. To get around it, you need to fill the block with your creativity.

TOP SECRET!
have someone from your family add a doodle to the block

Doodle a few of your favorite things inside the block.
It could be your favorite toy, food, or shoes . . .
anything that makes you happy!

Sometimes driving on the road gets super-boring! Besides telling jokes, Rainer really likes making creative doodles.
Draw some creative things just like Rainer.

draw a road sign you see

draw a word you see in your car

draw a building you see out of the window

draw some flowers you see

The Monstas passed through Rainbow Arch, marking the beginning of the Great Food Plains.
As you can imagine, Chomp was very excited!
Doodle some of the foods that might grow in the Great Food Plains and color in Rainbow Arch.

SUPER AWESOME!

Doodle your family's and friend's favorite foods.

GRANDMA

DAD

BFF

COUSIN

MOM

BROTHER OR SISTER

MONSTA TOONAGE
A DOODLTOON

What's up with Chomp?

Ever since he found out we would be coming through the Great Food Plains, he's been "training" at every stop.

GO! GO! GO!

draw your favorite food here

1...2...3...4...

Training for what?!

The Largest Hot Dog Known to All Monstakind. He's been doing pretzel pull-ups...

Whoa! Whoa! Whoa!

The jawbreaker balance walk...

draw designs on the jawbreakers

The Monstas pulled off the road to rest and play at the Giant Ice Cream Scoop Monsta Park.
Draw the giant scoop of ice cream and don't forget to add the sprinkles!

Draw all your favorite ice cream toppings on this billboard.

Welcome to the
Giant Ice Cream Scoop
Monsta Park where
Life is Sweet!

draw something for
Creely and Slogs
to sit on and eat their
ice cream

While visiting Chocolate Cup Canyon, the Monstas loved jumping and playing in the chocolate fountains and sliding down the chocolate slides.

Chocolate Cup Canyon is a messy place.
Have fun and make a BIG MESS on this page.

doodle a happy face

Chocolate makes my world go 'round

TOP SECRET!
get chocolate on your
fingers and smear
it on this page

Chomp was a little too excited for the factory tour at Squirmin's Gummy Worm Factory. He put the worm-making machine on hyperdrive, leaving a huge mess! Color and doodle your way through the gummies to connect the Monstas to Chomp.

Uhhh . . .

Welcome to Squirmin's Hall of Gummy Worms.
Draw the different kinds of gummy worms on display.

draw gummy worms on the shelves

Milkshake Mountains mark the end of the Great Food Plains. The mountains are home to Mount Monstmore, a monument dedicated to history's greatest Monstas.

Draw the missing Monstas from Mount Monstmore and the missing things around Milkshake Mountain.

draw a design on the cups

draw an animal looking at the Monstabego

draw a milkshake waterfall

draw
faces
on the
Monstas

The first Monsta to explore Gross Gorge went by the name Massive Monkey Man. He loved everything gross!

Doodle a monkey face on the statue
and extra gross doodles, too!

WARNING!

MONSTA
MESS INSIDE!

← copy this page then cut along the dotted line to make a poster →

We all get a little gross from time to time. It's always nice to
warn people when they are about to enter a gross zone.
Doodle a gross warning sign to hang on your door.

The Booger-Picking Musuem Hall of Fame displays all the greatest noses in the Doodlverse. Draw these noses.

cover the wall in doodles of stinky socks

Who knew there were so many stinky socks?

Must be where all the nasty missing socks go.

No kidding! It's unbearable.

STINKIEST SOCK SUPERSTORE

tee-hee   tee-hee

BAD

It's time for another joke with Rainer . . .

What's so funny?

You reminded me of a joke.

Let's hear it.

What kind of socks do bears wear?

doodle two big bear feet

Draw some of the smelliest things you can think of to hang on the walls of the Stinkiest Sock Superstore.

I DON'T TOOT
I SPARKLE

doodle a background for the Toots Trail

Toots Trail
(fill in the missing words)

Traveling from the Stinky Socks Museum to the Largest Ball of Belly Button Lint, the Monstas must _____ down
(a movement you make)
Toots Trail. As soon as they made it to the trail, Creely's

_____ began to rumble. The trail was covered in
(part of your body)

_____ and _____ , known for their
(something you drink)   (something you eat)

power. No matter how hard Creely tried, he couldn't get his

_____ to stop rumbling, and before he knew it, a
(part of your body)

_____ slipped out of his _____ .
(thing in your house)   (part of your body)

Tazza yelled, "_____ !"
(something yelled at a sports event)

Lovegood, a little shocked, said, "_____ ." All the
(a common saying)

Monstas burst into _____ .
(action)

"I didn't toot, I sparkled!" said Creely.

Doodle the Largest Ball of Belly Button Lint. It was pulled from a giant Monsta and put in the large hand statue, used to remind Monstas to clean their belly buttons.

doodle gross stuff in the belly button lint

Doodle all the gross things on the Largest Used Cotton Swab.

DeeWee added more pictures to his road trip photo album. This time, it's the marvelous creatures of the Magical Mystical Mountains.
Draw the creatures into the pictures.

draw a face on this Monsta

draw a gnome sitting on a mushroom

Now, that's magical!

draw a unicorn sitting in the clouds

The Yelling Yellow Yeti welcomes travelers to the Magical Mystical Mountains. He is known for his big mouth and super-loud yelling.

Draw his big mouth and what he could be yelling.

Be Happy!

TOP SECRET! draw something you yell that makes you happy on this page

Creely loves mini golf, and the Monstas stopped for a quick game at Mermaid Mountain.
Doodle the things around Mermaid Mountain.

Doodle clouds shaped like animals in the sky.

This is a really nice phone!

Do you know how mermaids talk with their friends?

No, how?

doodle what you think a shell phone would look like ↓

A SHELL PHONE

HA! HA! HA! HA!

Oh, boy.

VOTE check one ☐ good joke ☐ bad joke

Ms. Monty's Mythical Farm sends magical unicorn toots across the Doodlverse to Melvin's Magical Myths store.

Doodle these
in the magical
unicorn cloud

* sparkles *
* ice cream *
* cotton candy *
* rainbows *
* clouds *
* bells *

This is going
to be so
AMAZING!

Melvin's top-selling products are canned unicorn toots. Monstas use the magical spray for good luck and air freshener because unicorn toots smell like cotton candy!

Doodle a design on the label of the unicorn toots can.

MONSTA TOONAGE
A DOODLTOON

THIS HAS TO BE THE GREATEST DAY EVER!

BAD

It's time for another joke with Rainer. . .

This is going to be so AMAZING!

HEE! HEE!

HEE! HEE!

DUDE! It's just a bounce house.

It's not JUST a bounce house. It's a BUNNY bounce house!

doodle the bunny bounce house

doodle fun shapes around Tazza

Tazza is really into bouncing

Definitely! What do you say to a bunny who needs a ride?

Hop in!

Uhh.

doodle a bunny with big floppy ears

On the wall outside the bunny bounce house is a fun doodle mural. Fill in the missing letters to solve the word puzzles and draw the answers in the boxes. Then, find the hidden object in the mural and color it in!

f l o __ __ er   c __ r r o t   g h o __ t

p _ ncil   cam _ ra   b _ ok

FUN

TOP SECRET!
How many crayons
are hiding in the mural?

When the Monstas returned to the Monstabego, they found an invitation to the Supersilly Festival.
Draw a design on the invitation.

SUPERSILLY FESTIVAL

FREE TOUR:
Willie's Weird
Wardrobe Factory

FUN ACTIVITIES INCLUDE:
The Not-So-Super Superhero Party
Doodlverse's Ugliest Sweater Contest
Fantastically Funny Fun House Mirrors

While waiting in line to get into the Not-So-Super Superhero Party, Slogs was amazed by the fruit juice fountain.
Draw different types of fruit in and around the fountain.

MONSTA TOONAGE
A DOODLTOON

What a super party!

Who knew there are so many not-so-super superheroes!

It's time for another joke with Rainer...

BAD

I think it's great so many Monstas can be themselves!

Yeah! It's awesome.

Yeah, look, it's Unicorn Man!

doodle it

Over there, it's Cotton Candy Girl!

Ooo!

doodle it

THINGS THAT MAKE ME SUPER

VOTE check one ☐ good joke ☐ bad joke

The Fantastically Funny Fun House Mirrors are so much fun to stand in front of and make funny faces.

Draw your reflection in the mirrors, and make sure to add funny faces!

draw yourself with a wavy body

draw yourself with a really wide body

You're super-funny!

LET YOUR INNER MONSTA OUT!

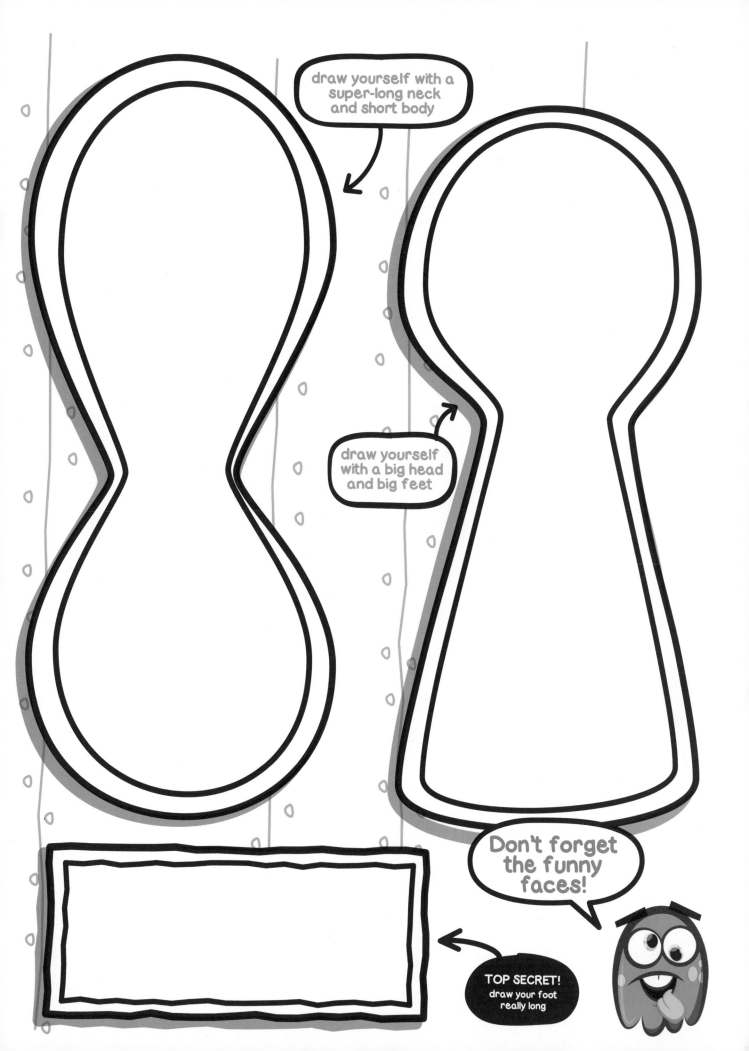

It's time for the Doodlverse's Ugliest Sweater Contest!

Doodle ugly designs on the sweaters. Follow the lines to figure out which Monsta's sweater you are designing.

While visiting Willie's Weird Wardrobe Factory, Tazza and Lovegood decided to try on some crazy costumes.

Draw the costumes on Tazza and Lovegood.
You can add anything you like to them!

Sir Doodlot's Kingdom is right around the corner, but first up is a stop at Pete's Pencil Palace. It was the perfect place to rest before Tazza made it to Sir Doodlot's and finally achieved his dream.

Draw some pencils with fun designs on this page.

imagine

**Next door to Pete's Pencil Palace is
Ernie's Eraser Emporium.**
Shade the box below with your pencil and use your
eraser to make a drawing.

The Monstas made the final turn off the highway, and Tazza was so excited to see Sir Doodlot's Kingdom in the distance.

Doodle the fun things around the entrance to Sir Doodlot's Kingdom, plus the super-magical castle.

doodle sold out sign

↖ doodle a ticket to Sir Doodlot's Kingdom

We've made it across the Doodlverse!
Draw a line connecting all the places the Monstas visited from start to finish, and draw a star next to your favorite place.

The Booger-Picking Musuem

Largest Used Cotton Swab

Massive Monkey Man

Gross Gorge

Mount Monstmore

Largest Ball of Belly Button Lint

Magical Mystical Mountains

Stinkiest Sock Superstore

Milkshake Mountain

The Yelling Yellow Yeti

FINISH

Sir Doodlot's Kingdom

Mermaid Mountain

Melvin's Magical Myth Store

MELVIN'S

Willie's Weird Wardrobe Factory

Pete's Pencil Palace

Ernie's Eraser Emporium

map of the
DOODLVERSE

The Monstas had a great time on the road trip and followed their dreams.
Doodle some of your dreams and how you can achieve them below.